Rota 4 22/4/13

BLACKBURN WITH DARWEN LIBRARY

This book should be returned to a
Blackburn with Darwen Library on or
before the latest date shown.

For Anna – welcome to the world! – KM
For my sister Laura – KJ

STRIPES PUBLISHING
An imprint of Little Tiger Press
1 The Coda Centre, 189 Munster Road,
London SW6 6AW

A paperback original
First published in Great Britain in 2013

Text copyright © Kelly McKain, 2013
Illustrations copyright © Katy Jackson, 2013

ISBN: 978-1-84715-247-3

The right of Kelly McKain, and Katy Jackson to be identified as
the author and illustrator of this work respectively has been
asserted by them in accordance with the Copyright, Designs and
Patents Act, 1988.

A CIP catalogue record for this book is available
from the British Library.

Printed and bound in the UK.

10 9 8 7 6 5 4 3 2 1

ANIMAL S.O.S.

THE CASE OF THE SECRET PONY

KELLY McKAIN

Illustrated by Katy Jackson

Stripes

MAP OF WHITE HORSE BAY

Vet's

Cliff-top Path

High Cliffs

Café

Beach

NOT TO SCALE

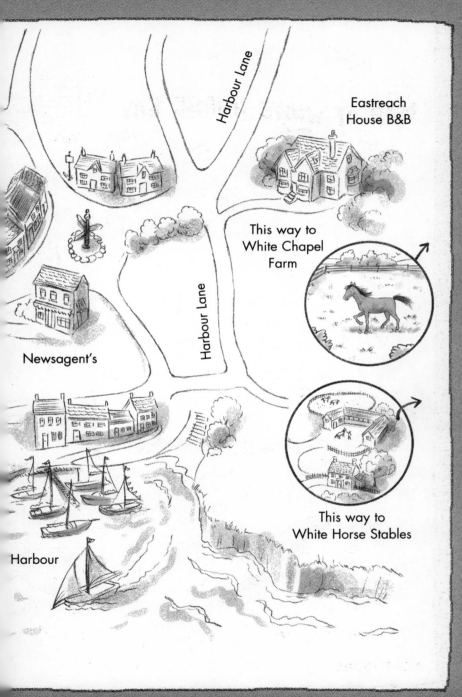

Harbour Lane

Eastreach
House B&B

This way to
White Chapel
Farm

Harbour Lane

Newsagent's

This way to
White Horse Stables

Harbour

CHAPTER ONE

Amy came staggering into the kitchen of the B&B with a huge stack of freshly washed sheets, towels and pillowcases balanced in her arms. "Mum, shall I put these in the airing cupboard upstairs," she asked, "or are they going straight back into the Swallow and Bluebird rooms?"

"In the airing cupboard, please," Mum replied. "Oh dear, I think this pipe's leaking. I'll have to get the plumbers back in."

Amy lowered the pile of laundry just enough to peek over the top, and found

Mum kneeling on the newly tiled floor, with her head in the cupboard under the sink. "What a pain," said Amy. "Oh, and speaking of pains, Mrs Kilbride in Starlings wants to know if there's any *damson* jam with breakfast?"

"Shhh!" Mum hissed, even though she couldn't help smiling too. "The customer is always right, remember? There's some on the middle shelf of the dresser. Put it into a nice little bowl with a spoon, though, don't just hand her the jar. Oh, but Amy, take the laundry up first, won't you, love? Jam and clean sheets don't mix!"

Amy smiled. "Sure."

When Amy and her mum had moved from London down to the small Cornish fishing village of White Horse Bay, the B&B had just been a building site. Now, here they were, up and running, and fully booked all through the summer holidays. Mum had

hired a chambermaid and general helper, a lady called Elaine, but she didn't start for another week. So Amy had been rushed off her feet helping out ever since she'd got back from school, where she was a weekly boarder. She now knew how to lay a table and make up a bed, and she could boil an egg – and cook a full Cornish breakfast, in fact! Even her bathroom cleaning had finally passed Mum's eagle-eyed inspection …
after the third try anyway!

As Amy shuffled carefully back through the doorway, Mum said, "You've got your riding lesson later this morning, haven't you, love? Why don't I drop you at the stables early and you can spend the whole day with Leah? I'm sure you're desperate for a catch-up."

"I'd love to," said Amy, thinking about her friend. "If you're sure you can manage without me."

"Of course I'm sure," Mum insisted. "It's been great having the extra help at weekends, but you're not spending your whole summer holiday working! Here, take this, for all the effort you've put in." She handed Amy a five-pound note from the jar on the window sill.

"Thanks, Mum," said Amy, tucking the money into her skirt pocket. "I'll just go and put these things away, and then I'll find that jam."

"Oh, and could you put some more little shampoos and shower gels in Chaffinch on your way back downstairs?" Mum asked. "Sorry. That's the last thing, promise."

"OK," said Amy. "I wish you'd gone with my idea of calling rooms after types of dogs, rather than birds, though," she added, with a grin. "Dogs are great. Hint, hint."

"You and your dog obsession!" Mum groaned. "Now go on, off you go!"

Half an hour later, Mum managed to get away for a few minutes to drive Amy up to White Horse Stables. Leah came racing over to meet them, with her dog Rufus bouncing along by her side. Amy had hardly got out of the car when Rufus leaped up to try and lick her face. Leah gave her a hug and cried, "Oh, Amy, it's so great to see you!"

"You too!" squealed Amy, squeezing her tight. "It's been over a fortnight, what with me being at Dad's last weekend!"

"Bye, love," Mum called, as she reversed the car. "I'd better get going, make sure there's nothing else Mrs Kilbride needs!"

"Bye!" Leah and Amy both called as she pulled away.

"Who's Mrs Kilbride?" asked Leah.

"Oh, no one, just a tricky customer," said Amy. "Anyway, I want to forget all about the

B&B today. It'll be so great for us to just hang out and relax."

"You're joking, aren't you?" Leah snorted. "I've got a list of jobs as long as my arm!" She held out her arm and waggled her fingers. "Mum's having a clear-up at the yard. She's got a big group of tourists coming for a hack this afternoon and she wants it all to look perfect. It's going to take me all day, unless…" She looked hopefully at Amy. "If you give me a hand we can be finished twice as quickly."

"Oh, go on then," said Amy, "as long as there's an ice lolly or something in it for me at the end. It's boiling today!"

"Deal!" said Leah. "Adam's still at cub camp, so there should be a few left in the freezer for a change. He usually scoffs the lot the second Mum gets back from the shops!"

Amy smiled. Adam was Leah's little

brother, and even *she* found him annoying. Leah pulled out a crumpled piece of paper from the back pocket of her denim shorts and peered at it. "Right, first on the list, sweep the yard."

As Leah and Amy went to the storeroom to get themselves some brushes, they passed Vanessa, Rani and Hayley, and they all greeted each other. Amy had seen the three girls around the stables when she rode, which was usually every other weekend, when she wasn't up in London staying with Dad. Now they were coming out of the tack room with saddles in hand, and bridles slung over their shoulders, ready to tack up for their lesson. They usually spent weekends at the stables, helping out. As they reached the yard, Amy saw someone she didn't recognize – a boy who looked a couple of years older than her. He was talking to Jane the new stable girl.

Amy was just about to ask who he was when Leah spoke. "Oh, that Billy's here again! He drives me mad, acting like he's the world's biggest expert on ponies!"

Amy watched as Jane handed him a pitchfork and gestured in the direction of the stables. "Ha ha!" cried Leah gleefully. "Looks like he's drawn the short straw with the mucking out! Serves him right after the way he was ordering me about yesterday."

"Does he help out here now then?" Amy asked.

Leah groaned. "Yes … unfortunately. He's George's mate." George was Leah's older brother. "Billy's so annoying!" Leah went on. "Yesterday he came over and checked whether I had Nutmeg's girth on tight enough – the cheek of it! OK, so he's got a bit of experience, but he really thinks he knows it all!"

"Poor boy!" cried Amy.

"What?" Leah shrieked.

Amy grinned. "Well, it looks like he's got on the wrong side of you, and I can imagine that's not a very nice place to be!"

Leah wrinkled her nose at Amy and handed her a brush. "If he wasn't so arrogant…" she began. Then, "Oh, here comes Mum – get sweeping!" she said hurriedly.

As Amy and Leah got to work, they filled

each other in on the final fun days of the summer term at their different schools, and Leah told Amy about the cinema night she'd had with her friends in Castlereach, the nearest town. "It's probably the last I'll see of them this summer," she added. "They all go off on holidays and things. I wish I was going somewhere! I bet you are, aren't you?"

"Yeah, a Greek island with Dad for a week," said Amy. "Sorry!"

"You're so lucky," moaned Leah.

"True. But then, you live on a stable yard all year round, and you've got your own pony and a dog!" Amy cried, nudging her. "I'd call that lucky!"

Leah had to smile. "I guess so. We'll just have to have some amazing adventures right here, won't we?"

Amy smiled back. "Well, the Easter holidays certainly were exciting," she admitted, "what with foiling those horrible property developers, finding new homes for all those kittens and rescuing Jester from the cliff!" She sighed, thinking about the little golden-coloured dog. "Oh, I still miss him. It was brilliant having a dog to look after, even if it was only for one night."

"I take it you haven't got anywhere with your mum on your getting-a-dog campaign then?" Leah asked.

Amy sighed as she swept a big pile of dust and straw into the dustpan that Leah was holding. "No, and it's less likely than ever now she's at full stretch running the B&B. There's already an endless round of cleaning and tidying to do. She's made it clear that the last thing she wants is a dog creating more mess."

"Oh well, you'll just have to share Rufus," said Leah, as he trotted up to them.

"Aw, thanks," said Amy. She made a big fuss of the shaggy brown dog and he sat

right down on the
dustpan and wagged
his tail, spreading
dirt everywhere
again.

"Rufus, you dufus!
Go on, off you go and
play!" Leah cried, shooing him away.
"I guess I can see your mum's point about
mess," she admitted.

Fifteen minutes later, the yard was
spotless and the girls were leaning on their
brushes, wiping their sweaty hair away from
their faces and admiring their hard work.

"There's not a single bit of straw on this
yard," Amy said proudly.

But then...

"Oy!" Leah cried, as Billy came out of
the stable block right in front of them,
pushing a full wheelbarrow. He was striding
along, headphones in his ears, jogging the

barrow about and tipping bits of muck and old straw everywhere.

"Stop!" cried Leah, leaping into his path and waving her arms, a furious look on her face. "Be careful, you idiot! Look what you've done!"

"All right, all right!" mumbled Billy, pulling a headphone out of one ear. "Don't get your knickers in a twist!" Then he put it back in, and carried on lolloping along, singing and dropping bits.

"I'll... he'll... you wait..." gasped Leah, so cross she couldn't even string a sentence together.

"Don't worry," Amy told her, "it's only a few bits. We can pick them up again."

"That's not the point," Leah grumbled. "I'm sure he did it on purpose, just to annoy me!"

"Oh Leah," Amy grinned. "He's really got under your skin, hasn't he?"

At that moment, George appeared from the tack room, grooming kit in hand, so he got the full force of his little sister's fury. "Why's that Billy here all the time? He's *your* mate, tell him to stop winding me up!"

George shrugged. "Actually, I hardly know him – he's in the year below," he told her. "We've played football a couple of times in the park and he came back with me after a kick-about one day because he's keen on horses, but it was Mum who said he could help on the yard in return for lessons."

"Well, tell him he can't!" Leah snapped.

"Leah!" cried Amy. "That's not fair!"

"No, I won't," said George. "He works hard round here and we need all the help we can get over the summer holidays. And he's quite experienced with ponies, too. Why does he bother you so much? Ooooh," he teased, his eyes twinkling. "Maybe someone's got a little crush!" Then he hurried off before Leah could thump him.

The girls made the yard perfect again, and then checked the time on Amy's phone. "Come on, let's go and get Nutmeg and Gracie in from the field," Leah said. "I can do some work on the lunge rein with Nutmeg while you have your lesson."

Amy felt that familiar excitement rise up inside her. She always got that feeling before a riding lesson, and she was almost skipping along as they went into the tack room to fetch a couple of lead ropes.

"Oh, where's my purple and blue one gone?" said Leah, rooting around in her grooming kit. "It's not here. That's weird. I tied it round the handle, same as usual, and now it's missing."

"Maybe someone borrowed it," said Amy. "You could use one of these instead. Here." She pulled a green lead rope out of the spares box and handed it to Leah.

"Yeah. Thanks," said Leah distractedly, taking it. "It is strange, though. I could have sworn I put it there. Oh well, maybe I didn't."

Half an hour later, Nutmeg and Gracie were in from the field and groomed, and Gracie was tacked up, all ready for Amy's lesson. As Vanessa's group walked their ponies back to the yard with Jane, Leah's mum, Rosie, came across to the barn from the manège, glugging from a huge bottle of water.

"Hi Amy," she said, as she reached her. "Are you and Gracie good to go?"

Amy nodded, as she did up the chinstrap of her hat. "I think I've remembered everything," she said. She'd wanted to try getting Gracie ready all by herself, so Leah hadn't helped at all.

"Hmm, let's see…" muttered Rosie, as she checked Gracie's tack and lifted her hooves. "Well done," she told Amy finally, "and her coat's beautifully glossy too."

"I gave it a good going over with the body brush," Amy said, feeling pleased that Rosie was impressed.

"Amy's got so much horse-sense now," said Leah, "and she can ride really well. We'd love to hack out on our own soon."

Amy blushed. Of course she was keen to hack out, but she hadn't expected Leah to ask her mum right then, with her standing there.

"I don't know about that," said Rosie, with a smile. "Amy's not quite ready. But I could come out with you both sometime this week if you like – how does that sound?"

"That would be amazing! Thanks Rosie," said Amy. Just thinking about it gave her butterflies in her stomach.

"First I need to make a quick call," said Rosie, and hurried off towards the office.

"And I'm just going to pop into the feed room," said Leah. "I've got some apples on the side in there for these two."

"I'll come with you," Amy said, tethering Gracie up and following Leah across to the feed room.

But once they were inside, Leah just stared at the counter. "Oh, *they've* gone too!" she gasped. "What is going on round here today?"

"Someone probably just used them without realizing they were yours," Amy said. "Oh, well—"

"But I wrote a note – look," said Leah, holding up a scribbled bit of paper that read, "Do not touch – for Nutmeg!"

Amy couldn't help grinning at that. "Calm down, it's only a few apples," she told her friend.

Leah sighed. "Yeah, you're right. It's not a big deal. Come on, it's time for your lesson."

CHAPTER TWO

"Hello, Amy," Rosie called from the yard.

Mum was dropping Amy off at White Horse Stables the next day.

"Hi," Amy cried. "Where's Leah?"

"Around here somewhere," said Rosie, heading into the office, so Amy set off to find her.

Leah wasn't in the tack room or the barn, or mucking out stables or grooming Nutmeg. And Rufus didn't bound up to Amy for his usual fuss and stroke – he seemed to have vanished too. Amy eventually tried the feed

27

room, stepping out of the bright sunshine and blinking as her eyes adjusted to the gloom. There was Leah, standing at the workbench holding a bunch of carrots, with Rufus beside her.

"What are you doing with those?" Amy asked.

Leah jumped and whirled round. "Oh! Hi, Amy! I'm setting a trap – to catch the thief!" she said gleefully.

Amy gasped. "Thief? What are you talking about? You don't think someone could have *taken* that stuff, do you?"

"Sure do," said Leah. "Usually I'd blame Adam – he'll do anything to annoy me. But he's still away and I asked everyone else about the apples last night – Mum, Dad, George and Jane – they all said they hadn't moved them, and none of them have borrowed my lead rope. Vanessa, Rani and Hayley are here again today ... and that Billy." Her face clouded over just saying his name. "And they were all here yesterday too, so it could have been one of them."

"Leah!" Amy cried. "You can't just go around accusing people of stealing! Anyway, even if those things *were* taken, you can't be sure it was one of them – a stranger could have wandered on to the yard."

"No way," said Leah firmly. "We all keep an eye out. If someone dodgy had been hanging around here, they would have been noticed."

"But there were tourists here as well yesterday," Amy pointed out. She grinned. "Maybe one of them got hungry!"

"Ha ha!" Leah retorted. "It's a different group of tourists today, so if these carrots go missing, that means the thief is either Vanessa, Rani, Hayley or Billy. And I know who my money's on."

"Leah…" Amy began, glancing nervously towards the door.

"If it's all such a crazy idea, then where's my curry comb?" Leah asked. "That's gone missing too. It was in my grooming kit this morning and now I can't find it anywhere."

Amy sighed. She still wasn't convinced, but she knew that if Leah had a bee in her bonnet about something, she wouldn't stop until she'd got to the bottom of things. "OK, OK, so what's the plan then?" she asked.

"Well, I made sure Vanessa, Rani, Hayley and Billy all saw me coming in here with these carrots," Leah explained. "So now I'm putting them on the workbench and if they're gone when I get back, I'll be able to trace who's taken them using my ace sidekick, super-dog detective Rufus to sniff them out!"

Rufus barked excitedly at this. Amy rolled her eyes. "He doesn't even sit when you tell him to!" she said. "How's he going to suddenly lead you to some fruit and veg-stealing master criminal?"

"Oh, come on, Amy," cried Leah. "You're not taking me seriously! This could be our next big investigation!"

"What, the case of the missing carrots?" Amy snorted. "It's not exactly Sherlock Holmes, is it?"

"Theft is theft," Leah said primly, then she put the carrots on the side, placed another

Do Not Touch notice on top and pulled Amy out into the sunshine. "Come on, let's bring the tack outside to clean. We can sit on that picnic bench by the barn. The thief will be able to see we're there, and know we can't see the feed room, giving whoever it is the perfect chance to sneak in."

"Leah, if you're this desperate for a bit of adventure, maybe you should take up rock climbing or something," said Amy, but she was smiling by then.

"Ha ha," said Leah. "There's a thief around, I just know it. And I'm going to catch him."

"Or her," said Amy.

"Or her," Leah repeated. Just then, Hayley walked by and Leah gave her such a huge smile and over-the-top hello, as if to act normal, that Amy had to drag her off to the tack room before Hayley could ask them what on earth was going on.

The girls got through cleaning and waxing six saddles and bridles before checking back on the feed room. When they finally did, to Leah's excitement, the carrots had gone. "See?" she said, raising her eyebrows at Amy.

Amy shrugged. "OK, I admit there's *something* going on, at least," she mumbled.

"Finally!" cried Leah. Then she turned to Rufus. "OK boy, it's your big moment." She took a little bit of carrot from her pocket and let Rufus sniff it. "Go find!" she told him, but he just looked at her blankly, then went back to bouncing about, panting and wagging his tail as usual.

Amy grinned and gave him a big pat. "Looks like we'll have to track down the carrots ourselves then," she said.

"None of the suspects have left the premises," said Leah, sounding like a TV police show, "so that shouldn't be a problem."

First, Leah made Amy giggle by having a good check round in the feed room itself, in case someone had stashed the carrots somewhere to pick up later. Then Amy followed her across the yard and watched her peer into the office. "I'll get Mum out of the way," said Leah, "then we can go and check out the girls' bags. They're on the benches in there."

"Leah!" Amy hissed. "You can't go rifling through people's private property!"

They watched someone stride into the office. "That's true," said Leah. "Well, not yet, anyway. Peter the feed man's just arrived. Mum'll be in there with him for at least half an hour now, sorting out our order."

Amy sighed. "Let's go and put that tack

away," she said.

They were just putting the bridles and saddles back on their pegs in the tack room when Leah spotted something. "Look, down there," she hissed to Amy, pointing at a rucksack hidden far back under one of the benches.

"Oh, that's probably just—" Amy began. But before she could say any more, Leah was down on the floor, using a lunge whip to try and poke the bag out from under the bench.

"Leah—" Amy began.

It was too late. Leah was down on her hands and knees. "Keep watch for me," she said, biting her lip and wiggling the bag out into the open. As Amy reluctantly stood by the door, Leah managed to grab the bag with her fingertips. Then she pulled it out and unzipped it. "Look!" she hissed. There, inside, were the missing carrots. She rummaged beneath them and pulled

out her curry comb. "The cheek!" she cried.
"When I find out who—"

"Someone's coming!" Amy hissed, hearing
footsteps. "Quick, put it back!"

Looking panicked, Leah fumbled with
the zip of the bag and shoved the whole
thing back under the bench. There was just
enough time for her to scramble behind the
huge stable door with Amy before whoever
it was walked in.

The girls had expected it to be someone popping in for tack. But instead they watched in amazement as the person got down on the floor and reached right under the bench to pull out the bag, then hurried off with it.

They'd seen very clearly who it was.

"Billy!" gasped Amy, as they peered out of the doorway and watched him striding off across the yard. "So you were right about him – he is trouble!"

"Course he is," said Leah. "Right, let's go and tell Mum and Dad what he's been up to. They'll definitely ask him to leave after this!"

"No," said Amy, taking Leah by surprise. "Well, not yet anyway. There must be a reason why he's taking these things – they aren't valuable or new. Let's see if we can find out what it is, shall we?"

"Well, OK," said Leah. "But look, he's getting on his bike, we'll have to hurry..."

The girls sprinted after Billy, grabbing Leah and George's bikes and helmets from the shed on their way. George came out of the farmhouse just at that moment. "Hey, what are you doing?" he asked them.

"Just borrowing your bike to go to the shop," Leah fibbed. "Tell Mum and Dad, could you?"

"All right," said George. "Get me some chocolate, though, OK?"

"Erm … sure," said Amy, as she climbed on. Then they rode off as fast as they could. They caught a glimpse of Billy turning a corner ahead and had to pedal like mad to catch up.

"Why would he take carrots?" gasped Leah, as they raced up a hill.

"Maybe he's making soup?" said Amy.

"You're still not taking this seriously, are you?" Leah cried.

"Yes, I am," Amy wheezed, "I just don't think…"

Just then, Billy glanced backwards. "Get down," Leah hissed.

"Leah!" Amy shrieked as her friend knocked her off-course and cycled them both into a bush. They brushed themselves down and got back on.

"Come on or we'll lose him," hissed Leah, setting off again.

"I'm going as fast as I can," panted Amy.

But the girls weren't quite fast enough. When they rounded the next corner, Billy was nowhere in sight.

"We lost him!" said Amy.

Leah shook her head, breathing hard.

"No, we didn't. He lost us. He saw us, I'm sure of it. And then he gave us the slip. Because he's up to something."

"What shall we do now?" Amy asked. "He could just be on his way home."

"Maybe," Leah admitted. "But let's carry on up this lane for a bit anyway. There are a few routes to the main crossroads, so we might be able to get ahead and cut him off."

Amy didn't think there was much chance of that, but she set off after Leah anyway. She had no idea where she was or how to get back to the stables, so she didn't really have any choice. They cycled around for about twenty minutes, but there was still no sign of Billy.

It was Amy who first spotted the pony. It was off in the distance, at the far side of its field. "Oh, look over there, what a gorgeous pony!" she cried.

"I love its long black mane," said Leah,
slowing down the brakes. "Well, I guess
we've lost Billy," she admitted as they
stopped to watch the pony for a while. It
was walking up and down by the fence,
shaking its head and snorting, and wouldn't
come when they called out. And the more
they looked at it, the more uneasy they felt.

"It seems really agitated," said Amy. "I

think we're scaring it. Maybe we should back off."

But Leah was already vaulting over the rusty old gate. "It does seem a bit nervous," she said, frowning. "You stay there, I'm going to try and get a closer look."

Leah started to walk slowly towards the pony, but it whinnied and reared up, and then bolted over to the far corner of its field.

"Leah, be careful!" Amy called out.

"Maybe I won't try and get near it after all," said Leah, hurrying back to the gate. "It's a he, by the way. It's a bit worrying that he was so scared of me when I wasn't even close to him, though."

"He looks like he needs a good groom," said Amy, "and a good feed, too."

Leah climbed back over the gate. "Come on, let's go along the lane a bit and see if we can get a better look at him."

They cycled slowly down to the edge of

the field and as they did, the pony moved
again, as far away from them as he could get.

"I think we should call someone," said
Leah. "He seems really nervous." When
Amy didn't reply, she looked up and found
her friend staring at something tied on to
the fence. It was a lead rope. A blue and
purple lead rope. "Hey! That's mine!" she
gasped.

"Thought so," said Amy, frowning. "But
what's it doing here?"

Leah pulled the rope from the fence. "If Billy took the other stuff today, that means he also took this, which means he has something to do with this pony," she said.

"That's a lot to assume from one lead rope…" Amy began.

But Leah wasn't listening. "What if the pony's his and he's not looking after it properly?" she cried.

"If the pony were his, he'd have all his own kit and he wouldn't have to take things from the yard," Amy pointed out.

"Steal things," Leah snapped.

"Borrow things," Amy countered. "Maybe he's been trying to help him."

"If he wanted to help him, he should have called the RSPCA!" said Leah.

Amy nodded. "True. Look, let's not jump to conclusions till we know the whole story. We need to talk to Billy." She pulled out her phone and checked the time. "Mum's coming to get me in twenty minutes, so we'd better get back. Why don't we come here again tomorrow? See if we can work out what's going on."

"But we can't leave him—" Leah began, giving the pony a desperate look.

"He's in a secure field, with plenty of grass and fresh water," Amy pointed out.

"Well, OK," Leah agreed, looking mournfully at the pony. "But just until tomorrow. If Billy hasn't got a decent explanation, I'm calling someone straight away."

"OK, deal," said Amy. And as they cycled back to White Horse Stables, even she had to admit that Billy had a lot of explaining to do.

CHAPTER THREE

"So how did this lead rope come to be in a field a mile away, if you didn't take it?" Leah demanded, waving it in Billy's face the next day.

"I don't know!" snapped Billy. "I don't know anything about a pony. I don't have to answer to you!" And with that he gave Leah an angry glare and strode off.

Amy and Leah looked at each other.

"That could have gone better," said Amy, with a sigh.

"Why won't he admit he knows that

pony?" said Leah. "And why's he lying about taking things, when we know he did?" They hadn't told Billy they'd seen his bag. They'd wanted to see what he said about the other things first.

"I have to admit it does all seem very strange," said Amy.

"Most importantly, if Billy knows about that pony, then why hasn't he called the RSPCA?" said Leah.

Amy shrugged. "I don't have the answers to any of this. Look, let's go back down to the field again now, and if we can't see anyone around to ask about the pony, we'll call the RSPCA ourselves, OK?"

"OK, definitely," said Leah.

The girls went to get out the bikes again and head straight down to see the pony. But as they were passing the yard office, Rosie came out and roped them into doing a few jobs to get everything ready for her next

group of tourists. Whatever part of the yard
they were working in, Billy always seemed
to be somewhere else, so they didn't get
another chance to talk to him.

When they finally finished the chores,
Leah realized that it was time to take
Nutmeg out. "He's got a busy afternoon
being ridden in lessons," she told Amy, as
they walked up to the field to get him. "You
don't mind if I ride him down to check on
the pony, do you? I won't see him all day
otherwise."

"Of course I don't," said Amy.

As they were about to
leave the yard, with
Leah mounted on
Nutmeg and Amy
on Leah's bike,
they noticed
Billy heading
off again.

"Oh, look! Here's our chance to find out what he's up to!" hissed Leah. "Come on!" She trotted Nutmeg down the driveway, with Amy riding along beside them. They were much closer to Billy this time – so close in fact that Leah had to bring Nutmeg back to walk a couple of times so they weren't spotted.

About halfway to the pony's field, though, they somehow still lost Billy. As they reached a junction that went left, right and straight ahead, they looked in every direction, but they couldn't spot him anywhere.

"I don't get it – he was only just ahead of us!" Leah cried.

Amy sighed. "Look, this is where we lost him before," she said. "I think we ought to forget Billy for now and head to the field. The pony is what really matters."

"OK," said Leah, though she still looked

put out about losing Billy.

About five minutes later, they reached the pony's field. Billy was nowhere in sight, but, strangely enough, neither was the pony.

Then, suddenly, they heard the clatter of hooves behind them. Amy whirled round. Leah tried to keep Nutmeg calm as he whinnied and skittered backwards. "Look!" she gasped. "It's the pony! He's got loose!"

The pony was prancing about in the road, snorting and shaking his head.

"What are we going to do?" Amy cried.

Just then, someone came rushing round the corner behind him.

Billy!

"You!" cried Leah, looking suddenly furious. "I knew you had something to do with this! Why did you lie to us, Billy? What have you done to the poor thing? He's absolutely terrified!"

"I haven't done anything to him!" Billy
yelled, striding towards the pony. "How
dare you—"

"Stop it, both of you!" Amy cried, trying
to take control of the situation. "We have to
get him back in the field. Quickly, before
he does himself an injury."

"OK," said Billy, calming down. "Look,
I got here and found him in the road.
Maybe now there are three of us we can
herd him into his field."

ANIMAL S.O.S.

Amy felt sick. The pony was big and wild and completely out of control. She didn't fancy standing near him and trying to get him back down the lane. She looked anxiously up at her friend.

"Just stay calm," Leah said. "And if you feel like you're in danger, move right out of the way, OK?"

Amy gave her a quick smile. "OK."

"Right, let's go for it," Leah called to Billy. "I'll bring Nutmeg forward and send the pony back towards you." She unclipped the lead rope from her saddle and threw it over to Billy. As he caught it, the pony whinnied and skittered sideways, even though it was nowhere near him.

"OK, you push him this way and I'll try and get near enough to get the rope on him," Billy told Leah.

Leah spoke soothingly to Nutmeg and walked him slowly forward. The pony backed away, towards Billy, and for a few seconds the plan seemed to be working. But then, a noise somewhere in the hedge startled the pony and he whinnied and reared up, forcing Billy to throw himself to the ground to get clear.

"Are you OK?" Amy cried, rushing to Billy's side, forgetting to be scared.

"Yeah, I think so," he groaned.

As Amy helped him up, the girls looked at each other in shock. Amy could tell that Leah felt out of her depth too, even if she'd never admit it. "Leah, maybe we should just call someone to help—" she began.

But then Leah seemed to pull herself together. "There's no time," she said. "We have to get this pony off the road before something comes round that bend. Billy, you go and encourage him forward, and Amy, you bike down to the other side of that bend and warn any drivers to stop. I'll try walking Nutmeg on behind the pony again."

"OK," said Amy, grabbing her bike and cycling towards the corner.

Nutmeg walked on and Billy stood just ahead of the pony, making little clicking noises and speaking gently to him. Slowly, he began to move forward, keeping a cautious distance, following after Billy.

"Great! Well done, keep going," said Leah.

"Thanks," said Billy, smiling a little.

The pony seemed to relax a bit. He put his head down and began to move closer to Billy. As Amy reached the corner, she glanced behind her and saw that it was working. She felt a sense of relief. They were almost level with the gate – they didn't have far to go until the pony was safe. But just as she reached the corner, a huge lorry came barrelling round it. It was so sudden she didn't have time to signal to the driver, and it was going so fast she was almost knocked into the hedge herself.

"Billy, look out!" she screamed.

She watched in horror as Billy dived into the hedge. The lorry only just missed the pony. With a loud screech, he reared up again and bolted past Amy. The lorry driver started beeping his horn angrily and swearing at them out of the window.

"Same to you, mate!" Leah yelled, as he passed her and Nutmeg from where they'd taken refuge on a grass verge. "You were going way too fast! We'll never get that pony back now!" She trotted Nutmeg up the lane to Billy and Amy. "Are you OK?"

"Yeah, I think so," said Amy, feeling very shaken up. "What a bad driver!"

"We have to get the pony back," Billy pleaded with Leah. "He's right on that bend. The next thing that comes round the corner could kill him!"

"I still think we should call someone—" Amy began.

But Leah didn't answer her. She just looked from Amy to Billy. "I think we can handle this. Nutmeg and I will go round the corner, and try to drive him back this way. Amy, you and Billy make a barrier just past the gateway so he can't go tearing off down the lane."

Billy gave her a grateful smile. "Thanks," he said.

Leah nodded slightly, then cantered Nutmeg along the grass verge, past the pony. Before he could bolt again, she turned Nutmeg and headed back towards him. By the gateway, Amy and Billy made themselves look as big as possible by holding Billy's jacket between them and spreading their arms wide.

Suddenly the pony was rushing forward, with Leah right behind him. Amy and Billy shared a terrified glance, but they stood their ground. The pony reached them, and Amy squeezed her eyes shut, expecting to be thrown into the air, or trampled under his thundering hooves. But a second later when she dared to look, she found that the pony had swerved into the field, and that she was still standing. Trembling from head to toe, but still standing.

"Are you OK?" asked Billy, and she managed the slightest nod.

Nutmeg clattered to a halt beside them and Leah dismounted, giving Amy a high-five. "We did it!" she cried.

Billy grinned at Leah, and Amy was pleased to see that, despite their differences, Leah grinned back. "Come on, let's secure that gate before he gets out again," he said.

The gate had snapped off its rusty hinges and been completely flattened by the pony, so they had to use Leah's lead rope to tie it back up on one side.

"What can we use to secure the other side?" asked Amy.

"How about one of my stirrup leathers?" Leah suggested.

"That's genius!" cried Billy. "I'm so relieved we got him back in safely. I couldn't have managed it without you."

"What a team!" said Amy.

"Don't think we're mates now, though," Leah warned him as she wound the stirrup leather round and round the gate and post and buckled them tightly together. "I want to know why you lied to us – about knowing the pony, and taking the things."

Billy glanced at Amy for support, but she didn't look happy either. "I stood up for you, but Leah was right all along," she told him.

Billy sighed deeply. "OK, OK, I'll come clean," he said. "I spotted the pony a couple of weeks ago. I thought he'd been abandoned at first so I've been coming to look after him. That's why I borrowed those few things. I was planning to bring them back, honest, and replace the apples and carrots."

"But why didn't you just tell us what was going on?" asked Amy, softening. "We'd have given you the food, and lent you the other stuff. And we could have helped you with the pony."

Billy grimaced. "Maybe I should have done," he admitted. "But the fact is, I thought *she'd* interfere." He nodded in Leah's direction.

"I would have done," Leah grumbled. "Because, unlike you, I would have put the pony's welfare first, and called the RSPCA."

She and Billy glared at each other.

"You don't even know what's wrong with him, and you go jumping in, making accusations... That's exactly why I didn't tell you!" Billy snapped.

"Well, do *you* know what's wrong with him?" Leah snapped back.

"No, but since I started looking after him, I've seen the owner a few times," said Billy.

"So you know who it is?" said Amy, surprised.

"Why haven't you asked what's wrong with the pony?" Leah demanded.

"I did try, at first," said Billy, "but she just had a go at me for hanging around. She seemed to think I was up to no good, said she'd call the police if she saw me here again. I've made myself scarce whenever I've seen her since then."

"Well, we need to ask her what's going on and sort this out," said Amy, taking charge. "And if you two don't stop arguing I'm going to have to knock your heads together!"

CHAPTER FOUR

"I think the owner lives down the road," said Billy reluctantly. "At the farm." He pointed into the distance to where a group of white buildings stood amongst the fields.

"OK," said Amy. "Then let's go."

They rode down the lane in silence, Billy and Amy on their bikes, and Leah jogging along on Nutmeg, in sitting trot without her stirrups.

"White Chapel Farm," read Amy, pointing to the sign on the gate. She glanced at Leah. "Remember we need to be polite."

"True. If we get chucked off the property, we won't find out anything at all," added Billy.

"Huh!" Leah huffed.

"Can I help you?" a voice called out from a shed as they approached and a slim, outdoorsy woman in overalls came striding up.

"That's her," Billy whispered to the girls.

"We came to ask you about the black pony," Leah called out. "Is he yours?"

"Yes, he is," said the woman. "What about him?" When she reached them, she peered at Billy and said, "You're that boy, aren't you? The one who was hanging around before. If you've—"

But Billy cut her off and quickly explained about the pony getting out.

"Oh no. Is he OK?" The woman looked really worried.

"He's fine," Amy assured her. "We got him into the field. There's not a scratch on him, amazingly."

"Oh, that's a relief," she gasped. "Thanks for coming to tell me, and for getting him back in. I'll go and check on him just as soon as—"

"Why's he so thin and scruffy?" Leah said suddenly. "You don't seem to be looking after him very well."

"What?" The woman looked surprised at first, then angry. "Look, thanks again, but I think you should go now," she said firmly. "This is private property. You've got no right to come round here, making judgements when I'm, when I'm—"

"She's sorry," Amy said quickly, glaring at Leah. "She didn't mean it like that. We're just worried about the pony, that's all."

The woman sighed and rubbed her face with her hands. "Aren't we all?" she said, looking suddenly exhausted. "That's why I rescued him."

Amy and Leah gaped at each other in surprise.

"You rescued him?" Amy gasped.

"Oh," said Leah, feeling very awkward. "Sorry."

The woman gave her a small smile. "You're missing a stirrup leather, I see," she said.

"It's holding the gate up," Leah told her. "Just a quick fix. It'll need a proper repair."

"Wait a second, I'll grab some tools and come down with you to Spark's field," said the woman.

Spark? So that was his name, Amy thought.

"I'm Anna, by the way," the woman told them as she came back out.

"I'm Amy, and this is Leah and Billy," said Amy as they set off for the field. When they got there, Spark whinnied as Anna approached, seeming happy to see her, but he still wouldn't come to them.

"I feel awful that he's so scruffy. I've tried to groom him, but he won't let me near him," Anna explained.

Billy nodded. "I've been trying to do the same thing, the last couple of weeks. I hope you don't mind."

Anna smiled. "Of course not."

"I can usually get him to come to me now," he said. "But only when I'm on my own. And the second I get the grooming brush out, he's gone again."

"That's exactly what I've found," said Anna.

As Anna got on with repairing the gate, she told them how she'd rescued Spark a few weeks beforehand from a livestock sale. "We don't have any horses," she explained. "But he was going crazy in the ring and no one was bidding. I was worried about what would happen to him if I didn't take him on. I thought he was just distressed by all the noise and clamour, and that with a peaceful environment, and time and rest, he'd calm down and recover. But that hasn't happened. He's still as wild as ever, and now my husband's threatening to send him back to the sales."

The girls and Billy looked horrified. "But you won't do that, will you?" Leah gasped.

Anna sighed. "I might not have any choice. That's where Spark caught me one time, kicking out," she said, pulling up one of the sleeves of her overalls and showing them a nasty bruise on her arm. "He didn't mean to, of course," she added. "He was just frightened. There are worse on my legs, and he nearly got me in the stomach once. My husband's worried that I'll get seriously hurt soon. He's not willing to let it go on much longer. I wish I'd been able to turn Spark around, but I didn't realize what I was taking on." She turned to Billy. "It sounds like you've had more success with him than I have." She stepped back and inspected her handiwork on the gate. "Right, I think that's done it. You can have these back now," she said, handing Leah the stirrup leather and lead rope.

"Thanks," said Leah. "I don't think my bottom could take sitting trot the whole way home!" They shared a smile then, and Amy caught Billy's eye and smiled too.

Billy leaned on the fence and made a clicking noise, to try and entice Spark over. The pony seemed to have got more used to them all being there, because this time, slowly and cautiously, he came. The others moved well back, and that gave him the confidence to go right up to Billy. Billy reached out very slowly and gently patted him on the neck. "There you go, boy. You're all right. See? You're fine," he said.

"He really trusts you," said Anna, smiling.

Spark snorted contentedly and nuzzled Billy's arm. Right at that moment, he looked just like any other pony.

"Despite all the bruises, I kept going with him because I'm sure there's a really nice pony underneath," Anna told them. "That's why I called him Spark, because I could see a spark of goodness in him."

"You're right, I'm sure you are," said Billy. "If only we could find a way to turn him round, perhaps he could be happy. Maybe now that you and I have made contact, we could work together to get him to calm down and trust people? It could be a whole new start for him." He turned and beamed at Anna.

Anna smiled back.

"I'm afraid that won't be possible," came a voice from behind them.

"Chris!" Anna cried. "This is my husband," she told Billy and the girls.

"I came down to find you," said Chris. "Enough is enough. Come on, Anna. We've talked about this – tomorrow that pony has to go to the rescue centre."

"But it's not your decision to make," Anna hissed. "We'll discuss this later!"

"I'm not having you get hurt any more," Chris insisted. "I'm sorry, love, but this has gone on long enough."

Billy's face crumpled. "But … but that means I won't see him any more," he stuttered. He looked absolutely crushed. Spark whinnied and nuzzled closer to him, as if he understood that he was about to lose Billy too.

Anna looked really upset. "Maybe *you* could take him on," she suggested desperately.

"I couldn't afford a pony!" Billy cried, making Spark leap away from him. "And I've got nowhere to keep him."

"You're not really going to give Spark up, are you?" gasped Leah.

Anna looked devastated. She glanced at Chris. "I'm sorry, but what else can I do?"

Billy glared at her, looking really upset. Then he leaped on his bike and pedalled away.

CHAPTER FIVE

Leah and Amy had already been back at White Horse Stables for about half an hour when Billy turned up.

"I didn't expect to see *him* again today," said Amy, as he came marching towards them, rucksack in hand.

"Me neither," said Leah.

As he reached them, Billy scowled and shoved the rucksack at Leah. "Here's your stuff back," he said. "I've got no use for it now."

"Thanks," said Amy, but Leah just tutted

and looked into the bag. Amy peered in too – as well as the curry comb and body brush that had gone missing, there was a hoof pick, a small bag of pony nuts, several more brushes and a head collar.

"I suppose you're going to tell your mum I took the stuff and get me banned from the yard," Billy mumbled.

Leah sighed. "I should do, but no, I'm not going to say anything about you taking these. I know you were trying to help Spark."

Even that didn't seem to cheer Billy up. Ever since Anna's husband had said Spark had to go to a rescue centre, Amy had been trying to think of ways that Billy could keep him. Now she found herself blurting out, "Leah, maybe you could ask your mum if Spark could come to live here?"

For a moment Billy looked hopeful, but Leah shook her head. "I thought of that,

but there's no way Mum would have a pony
like Spark, with such behavioural problems,
on the yard. Not with clients around.
There's no point even asking."

Billy scowled at her again. "You mean,
you don't want to help me so you *won't*
ask," he said.

"Don't be silly," Amy said.

"It's not about you, idiot," Leah cried.
"It's a safety issue!"

"Oh, so you're in charge round here now,
are you?" Billy snapped.

"What's wrong with you three?" hissed a
voice behind them.

They all whirled round to find Rosie
glaring at them, hands on hips.

"I've got clients here, in case you hadn't
noticed!" she snapped, gesturing at the
group of tourists milling about the yard.
"In there, right now, all of you!"

The girls and Billy trudged moodily into

the office. Once they were sitting on one of
the benches, Rosie demanded to know
what was going on. Reluctantly, they ended
up telling her the whole story – about Billy
finding Spark, about how the pony had
been rescued from the sales, but was
impossible to handle, and about how he'd
almost been run over (they toned that bit
down – a lot!). Finally they finished on
meeting Anna and her husband and how
they were going to be sending Spark to a
local rescue centre.

"That seems a good solution," Rosie said.

"But it means I'll never see him again," Billy said quietly.

Rosie sighed. "I'm sorry, love. I can see that's upsetting, but I don't think there's really any other option. Although, actually … I do know of a specialist charity that looks after disturbed horses and ponies. Maybe that would be better for Spark than a rescue centre. This charity would be able to give him the long-term help and special care he needs. I could ring this Anna and tell her about it. I don't suppose you've got her number?"

"No, but she lives at White Chapel Farm," said Amy. She could still picture the name clearly in her mind, painted on the gate.

"Well remembered," said Rosie. "Although, perhaps I'd better call the charity first," she said. "Make sure they have a space before I get Anna's hopes up. Now, where's that article I read about them..." She rummaged around in a pile of horsey magazines on the tea-making table. "Ah, yes – here it is. The Second Chance Horse and Pony Charity. They're in Yorkshire..."

"Yorkshire," echoed Billy. "But that's the other end of the country..." Still, he stayed to listen in with Amy and Leah while Rosie rang up. "Hello?" she said, "I'm calling on behalf of my daughter, and her friends. They've come across a pony, a gelding called Spark, who's about to be sent to the local rescue centre by his owners because they can't cope with him. The thing is, from what they've told me, he's so distressed and his behaviour is very disturbed that I was hoping you might be able to take him instead. With your specialist environment, I thought you'd be the ideal place for... Yes, yes, that's right, yes... Of course – I just wanted to speak to you first, because if there was no possibility... Absolutely..." Although Billy and the girls listened intently, they couldn't quite work out how the conversation was going.

Rosie said "yes" and "no" a lot more, and "thank you", and when she hung up she told them that someone from the charity could come down and collect Spark in a week, if Anna agreed, of course.

"It really is the best thing for him," Amy said gently to Billy, but he wouldn't meet her gaze.

Rosie got Anna's number from directory enquiries and gave her a call, but from what Amy could hear, their conversation didn't seem to be going very well. Rosie was frowning a lot and saying, "Hmm, yes, well, I can understand that but, hmm ... I suppose that's the only option..." Leah and Amy looked anxiously at each other – what on earth was going on?

Rosie put the phone down and sighed deeply. "It seems Anna can't wait a week for Second Chance to collect Spark," she told them. "And the local rescue centre hasn't got room for him. So her husband's taking him back to the sales first thing in the morning."

"The sales?" cried Billy. "No way, he can't do that!"

"I won't let him!" shrieked Leah. "I'll tie myself to Spark's gate!"

"Calm down, both of you!" cried Rosie. "I couldn't let him do that either, though I wouldn't go as far as tying myself to the gate!" She took a deep breath. "I've agreed that we can have Spark here for the week until Second Chance can come and pick him up. It's not ideal when we're so busy, but what else could I do?"

"Oh, Mum, that's brilliant, thank you!"

cried Leah. She and Amy both leaped on
Rosie, hugging her tight
and thanking her
over and over again.

But Billy wasn't
celebrating. "I'm
going to… I think
I've got something
in my eye," he
muttered, and
stumbled out of
the office.

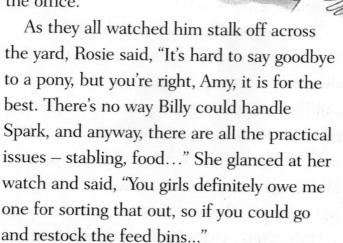

As they all watched him stalk off across
the yard, Rosie said, "It's hard to say goodbye
to a pony, but you're right, Amy, it is for the
best. There's no way Billy could handle
Spark, and anyway, there are all the practical
issues – stabling, food…" She glanced at her
watch and said, "You girls definitely owe me
one for sorting that out, so if you could go
and restock the feed bins…"

Leah groaned, but Amy just thanked Rosie again and dragged Leah out of the door. As they walked over to the feed room, Amy said, "I do know it's for the best, but I'm still really upset for Billy that he's got to give Spark up."

"I know," said Leah. "And I'm sorry I was so hard on him before. But I've been working out a plan – a plan that would mean Billy wouldn't have to lose Spark…"

"Leah, what are you on about?" asked Amy.

"Let's go and find Billy and I'll tell you," said Leah, looking around to make sure they weren't being overheard.

Billy was as surprised as Amy had been when Leah pulled him out of the tack room and marched him round to the hay barn. "What's going on?" he cried.

"I've got a plan," said Leah. Amy wanted to add, *Don't get too excited, though*. Leah's plans weren't always very practical.

Billy was staring at Leah in surprise. "Go on," he said eagerly.

"Well, how about we use the few days we've got with Spark till he leaves to rehabilitate him ourselves?" said Leah, her eyes sparkling. "Then maybe he won't actually have to go. Maybe we can persuade Mum to let you keep him here on livery."

"Livery?" said Billy. "You mean where I work on the yard to pay for Spark's keep?"

"Exactly," said Leah.

"Erm, sorry to put a downer on this, but what makes you think your mum's going to agree to that?" Amy asked. "And even if she did, why would you succeed where Anna has failed?"

"Well, Spark responded really well to Billy, remember," Leah reasoned. "If we all work together, we might be in with a chance."

"It's certainly an idea," said Billy cautiously. "Maybe my parents would be OK with me keeping Spark if I worked to pay the costs, and if they knew your mum was on-board. So, what do you think we'd need to do to convince her?"

Leah frowned. "It won't be easy," she admitted. "As well as being safe to handle in the stables and on the yard, Spark would have to be usable in lessons."

Billy looked nervous about that. "But we don't even know if he's rideable yet."

Leah frowned. "If we could show Mum you can ride him, then maybe that would be enough to start with – hopefully," she told him. "So long as she sees progress and potential, she might agree to him staying." She turned to Amy. "That's where you come in," she told her. "Mum'll want to see that Spark can be ridden in a group situation. You'll have to ride Gracie whilst Billy rides

Spark, and I'll ride Nutmeg."

"Of course, no problem," said Amy, feeling excited about helping out with a training programme. She was pleased with finally getting to ride in a group too, as she always had her lessons alone.

"So you're both in, yeah?" asked Leah.

"Yes," said Amy and Billy at once.

"Great," said Leah. "Not a word to anyone though, not even George. We'll have to do the training in secret. If Mum and Dad find out about this, they'll say it's dangerous and put a stop to it before we've even started."

Amy was about to ask Leah how she planned to train Spark in secret on such a busy yard and with only a week before Second Chance came to collect him, but Billy began to speak. "Leah, I just want to say sorry for being so off with you before. And thanks for all this."

"That's all right," said Leah. "Don't forget

I'm in charge, though," she added, with a cheeky smile. "You have to listen to me and do what I say."

Billy smiled. "OK, well, I'll try, anyway," he told her, grinning back. "Look, I'd better get going. Thanks again, for everything. And see you tomorrow, for Operation Spark."

CHAPTER SIX

When Amy arrived at the stables the next morning, she was even more excited than usual because they were collecting Spark from Anna's. Not only that, but her mum had agreed that she could stay the night with Leah.

Leah's dad, Dan, greeted Amy, then she ran up to Leah's room, where she found her friend lying on the bed surrounded by articles about pony training she'd torn out of horsey magazines. Amy put her stuff down and, after saying hello, they hurried downstairs, passing a cheeky-looking Adam on the way.

"Yes, he's back from cub camp, I'm afraid," Leah grumbled to Amy then cried, "Oy, get off!" as he tried to trip her up.

Out on the yard, the girls found Billy climbing into the Land Rover, which Dan had hooked up to the horse box. Rosie and George were already inside, too.

"Let's go and get this pony then!" said Rosie, as the girls dashed over and squeezed into the tiny back seat with Billy.

When they arrived at Spark's field, they found Anna ready and waiting. With Billy's

help, she managed to get a head collar on him. Billy clipped on a lead rope and after a lot of skittering about and backing away, and some gentle words, Spark finally let Billy lead him out of the field. He wasn't keen on going in the horse box, though. "You girls, stand either side with your arms out," said Rosie.

"Oh, good," Amy whispered to Leah, "I'm a human shield again!"

"Billy, lead him back round and then try to bring him up the ramp in trot," Rosie continued. "If he has less time to think about backing out, he might just go in."

It worked, on the third try. Anna thanked them again and said a tearful goodbye to Spark.

"You're doing the right thing," Rosie assured her. "He'll have somewhere safe to live at Second Chance where his behaviour will be understood. It really is the best place for him."

"I know, and that's great," sniffled Anna, "but I wish he could just be a normal, happy pony, getting to be ridden and having a friendship with his owner."

Billy and the girls glanced at each other. That was exactly what they were hoping for too. And they had a secret plan to try and make it happen!

Getting Spark into the horsebox had been challenging enough, but getting him back out at the stables was a nightmare.

"It must all be so new and different for him," said Leah. "The smells, the sounds."

Billy almost managed to lead Spark out on the first try, but then a wheelbarrow clanking past sent him cowering back in again. He refused to move when he heard the hay delivery truck reversing in the car park too.

When they did finally get him out, Rufus's excited barking sent him skittering across the yard.

"Hey! Whoa, boy!" Billy cried as Spark reared up, forcing him to let go of the lead rope.

"I've got it!" cried Amy. She made a grab for it, which startled Spark and she ended up being dragged through a flowerbed. And then when Leah tried to help her by diving for the rope herself, Spark kicked out in fright and caught her on the thigh with his hoof. She let out an ear-piercing screech and hopped about. "That really hurt!" she squeaked, going bright red in the face. "I can understand how Anna felt now!"

While Billy and George managed to get hold of Spark again, Rosie rushed over to Leah, to inspect the damage. "That's going to be a huge bruise, I'm afraid," she frowned. "What on earth have we got ourselves into? Oh well, he can go out in the field until Second Chance come on Monday. Thank goodness he's only here for a few days."

"She's taken against Spark already," Billy whispered to Amy. "It'll take a miracle to convince her to let him stay."

Early in the afternoon, Billy and Amy were
sitting on the fence watching Spark
grazing in the field.
Rosie had roped
off an area to
keep him on his
own, until they
were sure he'd be
OK with the other
ponies.

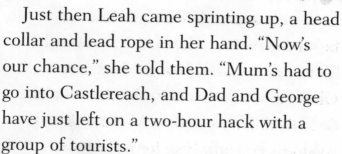

Just then Leah came sprinting up, a head
collar and lead rope in her hand. "Now's
our chance," she told them. "Mum's had to
go into Castlereach, and Dad and George
have just left on a two-hour hack with a
group of tourists."

"But Jane's around, isn't she," Amy asked.
"Surely…"

"She's busy in the office doing some

college coursework," Leah told her. "It's due in tomorrow. Mum said she could get on with it while things are quiet."

She handed the head collar and lead rope to Billy. "You go and get him in," she told him. "We can use the second manège – you can't see it from the yard."

So Billy walked across the field, making a clicking noise and calling to Spark. Amy watched anxiously, waiting for something terrible to happen. But after a few minutes, they were all amazed to see the pony turn and walk towards him. Billy slipped on the head collar and clipped the lead rope to it. "Well done, boy, I'm so proud of you," he said, giving Spark a pat on the top of his back.

But then, with a huge whinny, Spark suddenly reared up, only just missing Billy's face with his front hooves. He pranced about, bucking, and as Billy tried to calm him, he caught his leg, sending him flying. As Billy hit the ground, Spark skitters all around the field, snorting and shaking his head. "Oh my gosh!" gasped Amy, rushing across the grass to Billy, while Leah dashed over to try and calm Spark.

Amy helped Billy up. He was limping so badly, Leah rushed over to help him too. They turned to head back to the gate ... and saw someone running towards them, looking furious and very worried.

"Mum's back early!" Leah gasped.

"Billy, are you OK?" Rosie cried, reaching them.

"Fine, just a bruise," Billy muttered, letting go of the girls and leaning on the fence. He looked really pale and shaken up.

"What on earth is going on here?" Rosie demanded, glaring at Leah.

"Erm, well, we just thought ... if we trained him a bit..." she mumbled.

"You thought what?" Rosie shrieked. "You know how dangerous that pony is! And what did you think you were training him for anyway? He's off to Second Chance in a few days." Amy and Leah glanced at each other, but neither of them dared tell Rosie their plan. "Even worse, you went behind my back!" Rosie fumed. "I assume your father and George didn't know about this, either?"

Leah grimaced and shook her head.

Then Rosie turned to Amy and Billy. "You

two are in my care. I trusted you to be sensible while I went out for half an hour. When I think what could have happened…"

Amy blushed bright red and stared at the ground – getting told off by someone else's mum was just awful. "Sorry," she said quietly.

"Yeah, sorry," Billy and Leah mumbled.

Rosie sighed loudly and rubbed her face with her hands. "Look, is your leg all right, Billy?"

Billy nodded.

"OK, right, let's move on then," said Rosie. "You don't go anywhere near Spark from now on, understand?"

They all nodded.

"Good. Now, you three obviously need to be kept out of trouble, so you can go and stack up those new hay bales in the storage barn."

Billy and the girls stood watching as she stomped back down the track.

"It's hopeless," Amy said finally, with a sigh. "We'll have to give up on the plan."

"You're right," said Billy. "If we can't work with Spark…"

They both looked at Leah, hoping she'd have some clever idea, but she just seemed as defeated as they did.

Leah woke suddenly from her dream and sat bolt upright in bed. She saw from the clock that it was half past eleven. Amy was fast asleep in her sleeping bag on the fluffy rug, with Rufus beside her. They'd watched DVDs and eaten popcorn, and tried to stay up until midnight, but they'd been far too tired to manage it. Leah ran the dream back through her mind. She sensed it was important somehow, but she couldn't work out why. "Psst! Amy! Are you awake?" she hissed.

Amy stirred, then opened her eyes. "Well, I am now," she whispered. "What is it?"

"I've had a dream—" Leah began.

Amy groaned. "Leah, couldn't you wait until—"

"No, listen!" cried Leah, her voice full of excitement. "It was about Spark. I was riding him in the manège except, well, it started off as Spark and then he changed into Marley, this lovely chestnut we used to have here."

"Marley?" said Amy. "What made you think of that pony in particular?" She sensed that the dream was important too.

Leah shrugged. "I don't know."

"Well, OK, you said he used to be here. What happened to him? Maybe that's the key?"

"One of the riders took such a liking to him that her parents asked to buy him for her." Leah looked thoughtful. "He went off to his new home over a year ago."

"OK," Amy said. "But that doesn't explain why he changed places with Spark in the dream. Is there anything else you can remember at all?"

"I was riding in my pyjamas," said Leah.

Amy smiled. "I don't think that means much," she said. "Was there anything special about Marley in real life?"

Leah thought for a moment. Then suddenly she gasped and clapped her hand to her mouth. "I know! I know what it is!" she cried. "It was just a small thing, but one day, when Marley was still a riding school pony, someone started brushing him as usual and he just went completely crazy, rearing up and kicking out."

Amy sat up, too, then. "You mean the same as how Spark acted when Billy patted him today?"

"Exactly," nodded Leah. "And as it turned out, Marley had a trapped nerve in his back — it was causing him terrible pain. That's why he went so wild. Spark could have the same thing!"

"You mean, there could be an explanation for Spark's problems after all?" Amy cried. "Maybe something we could fix?"

"Well, we could at least get the horse osteopath to come and have a look," said Leah. "It worked for Marley. I'll ask Mum about it in the morning."

"That's so exciting!" Amy gasped. "Well, there's no way I can sleep now!"

"Me neither," said Leah. "Come on, let's go and get some hot chocolate and biccies."

At the mention of biscuits, Rufus obviously decided he couldn't sleep either, and instantly leaped up and followed the girls down to the kitchen.

As it turned out, they didn't have to wait until the morning to talk to Rosie about Spark, because she was still up, pottering around at the counter in her dressing gown. She made the hot chocolate for them, while Leah explained about her trapped nerve theory.

"It does sound plausible," said Rosie, stirring their drinks. "The trouble is, osteopaths are very expensive. Maybe we should wait for Second Chance to come and get Spark. I'm sure they have their own people…"

"But, Mum, if he's in pain—" Leah began.

Rosie sighed. "Frank, the osteopath who came to look at Marley, well, he did say he liked challenging cases…"

"And Spark certainly is that," said Amy.

Rosie sighed. "I'll call him tomorrow and see if he'll come over as a favour, just to give an initial assessment. That's the best I can do, I'm afraid."

"Thanks, Mum," said Leah, giving her a big hug.

Rosie hugged her back and then pulled Amy in too. "What were you girls thinking of, working with Spark today?" she asked, taking them by surprise.

Leah and Amy shared a glance. They knew they had to come clean. "Promise not to go mad, OK?" Leah said.

"Oh dear, I don't like the sound of that," said Rosie, handing them a steaming mug each, "but I'll try my best."

Leah took a deep breath. "We thought that … well, we thought that if we could sort out Spark's problems…" she began. She and Amy told Rosie all about their plan to get Spark to calm down and trust people. How they'd thought that if they could get him used to being handled and ridden, then maybe she'd let Billy keep him at White Horse Stables on livery. Rosie listened intently, looking more and more surprised with every word.

"Well, thank goodness I came back when I did!" she exclaimed.

"Sorry we didn't tell you earlier," said Amy.

"We thought it was hopeless, after today," Leah said. "But if Spark does have a trapped nerve and it can be sorted out, then could Billy keep him?"

"Hang on, you're getting ahead of yourselves here," Rosie told her. "The trapped nerve idea is a longshot. And even if that is the problem and Spark really settles down, Billy might not want to work for his livery."

"But he does!" cried Leah.

Rosie sucked in her breath. "Well, I'd have to be convinced that Spark was completely safe before I'd even think about him staying, and Billy's parents would have to agree," she said. "There are so many reasons why it might not work out."

"But you're not saying definitely no, are you?" said Leah.

Rosie frowned. "I'm saying we'll all have to take it one step at a time. Now, off you go to bed, you two, and get some sleep."

CHAPTER SEVEN

"Hello Frank, is that you?"

It was the next morning and Rosie was on the phone to the osteopath from the yard office. "Uh huh ... yup ... you can? That's great!"

A few seconds later, Rosie said goodbye and put down the phone. Just as she was telling Amy and Leah that Frank had agreed to come out and look at Spark, Billy walked in.

"What's going on?" he asked. Amy could tell he was anxious, but when she explained about the trapped nerve idea and the osteopath and how there might be hope for Spark, he got very excited.

Rosie kept them busy with chores over the next hour until Frank – a cheerful, heavy-set man in a checked shirt – arrived. They all headed up to the field and Frank caught Spark and got a lead rope on him as easily as Billy had done. He asked Rosie to hold him while he examined his teeth and hooves. As he looked at Spark from all angles, and watched him walk and trot, Rosie talked soothingly and kept him calm. Then Frank began to move his hands over Spark's back, and they all waited for the pony to go crazy, but he just twitched a little.

Rosie rubbed Spark's nose and smiled as he snorted and nuzzled into her. Leah and Amy shared a smile too – perhaps she was taking to him after all.

"Well, you were right about the trapped nerve," said Frank, after a few more minutes.

"Yes!" cried Leah.

"Can you free it?" asked Billy anxiously.

"I should be able to," said Frank. "Let's see…" No one spoke as they watched him work on Spark's back, pressing his hands down in different places and rubbing the muscles, like a massage. It didn't seem like much was happening, but then Frank stood back and said, "I think that should improve things. Let's look at him on the move again."

Well, even Amy could see the difference in Spark. He seemed more relaxed and this time he loped along in a much more fluid way. And he was so calm that after a while, Rosie even let Billy hold the lead rope and trot him up and down.

"Oh, thank you so much!" cried Leah.

"He's like a different pony already," added Amy. "You've worked a miracle."

Frank smiled. "Well, I wouldn't say that," he told them, "but it's great to see him moving nicely again. You just keep working with him like that, Billy, and he'll soon be back to his old self."

"I will," said Billy, grinning. "Thank you so much."

They let Spark off in the field, then walked back to the yard with Frank, still thanking him over and over again.

"I'll come back and check on him tomorrow, make sure things have settled down enough for him to be ridden," he told them. "For now, some gentle exercise on the lunge rein would really free up those stiff muscles and get him moving even better."

Of course, the second they'd waved Frank off in the car park, Leah turned to Rosie. "Can we lunge Spark, Mum? Please!"

"I've got a lesson to teach," Rosie told her, "and your dad's with the farrier. If George agrees to supervise you, it should be all right, though. But no trying anything silly, OK? I'll be right in the next manège, watching."

"Great, thanks, Rosie!" cried Amy. Leah and Billy thanked her, too, and then they hurried off to find George.

It took the promise of a batch of Amy's delicious cupcakes and Leah taking over his household chores for a week to get George on-board, but soon he was walking back down the lane with them to fetch Spark from the field.

Animal S.O.S.

As Billy led Spark to the manège, with Amy and George beside him, Leah slipped off and came back with a lunge line. "I'll start off and then when he's going nicely, you can have a go," she told Billy.

"Great," he said.

Billy talked to Spark gently as Leah clipped the lunge line to his head collar, and then he went to stand behind the fence with Amy and George. Leah got Spark walking in a circle round her, using the lunge line and a whip to guide him. Soon he was moving in a nice, relaxed way. She made some clicking noises and encouraged him to change pace. After a moment, he picked up a smooth, even trot. Amy thought it might have been her imagination, but he seemed to look very pleased with himself.

"He's doing brilliantly," said Billy, as Leah brought Spark back to walk, turned him

111

and got him to go in the other direction.
Then she called Billy over and handed him
the lunge line and whip, and soon he'd got
the hang of moving Spark round on the
circle. "He seems to know what I want him
to do," he said, grinning.

"You're doing really well," George told him.

"Looks like he's enjoying himself too,"
Amy added.

"He's obviously been worked with before," said Leah. "That means he's probably been ridden before too."

Billy and Amy smiled at one another. Now that Frank had worked his magic, maybe training Spark wouldn't be so impossible after all.

"I think we should leave it there for today," said Leah, after a few more minutes. "We don't want to tire him out too much."

Billy brought Spark to a halt and made a big fuss of him. As they walked past Rosie's lesson on their way back to the field, she came to the gate.

"Didn't he do brilliantly?" cried Amy.

"Frank has made a huge difference," Rosie admitted. "Spark's much calmer, and he looked far more comfortable on the move."

"So, can Billy keep him here on livery?" asked Leah eagerly.

Rosie laughed at that. "Well, I'm not saying no, but it'll take more than a bit of lunge-rein work to prove to me that he's safe. I'll want to see how he is at being handled round the yard, and to watch him being ridden in a group…"

"See, told you," said Leah to Amy and Billy.

"And I'll have to assess him on a hack out, to see how he is in the open," Rosie finished.

Leah, Amy and Billy shared a nervous glance. They hadn't thought of that one. Anything could happen out on a hack. Who knew how Spark would behave?

"I'll give you till Saturday," Rosie said. "You can show Dan and I how much Spark's improved then."

They all looked horrified at that. "Saturday?" Leah gasped. "But that's not very long. Can't we have a few weeks?"

"No, because, and it's not very likely, but *if* we decide Spark can stay, I'll need to ring and cancel his place at Second Chance," Rosie explained. "They're all set to come on Monday. I'd have to give them some kind of notice if we don't need them. They've been so kind to offer him a place, I don't want to mess them around. Now we've got to the root of the problem, a few days should be long enough to get him up and running, and assess his temperament." Then she turned to Billy. "And I'd need to discuss it with your parents, of course," she told him. "I think you should call now and fill them in on all this. There's no point getting your hopes up if they're only going to say no anyway."

"OK," said Billy. "I'm sure they'll be fine with it, though, seeing as I can work to pay Spark's way."

"*If* he passes the test," Rosie warned. "Come into the office when you've taken him back to the field. We can call them from there."

The girls and Billy thanked George for supervising them and then walked Spark back up to the field.

"Saturday?" said Amy. "That's in three days' time. Spark can't even be ridden until tomorrow and that's if Frank gives him the all clear."

"We have to try, we just have to," Billy insisted.

"I know," said Leah. "We really will give it our best shot!"

CHAPTER EIGHT

By the time Mum had managed to get away from the B&B the next morning to drive Amy up to White Horse Stables (with a box of cupcakes for George on her lap), Frank had already been back and pronounced Spark fit to ride. Billy's parents had agreed to think about keeping Spark, if he passed the test on Saturday – and they were coming to watch then too.

"He's been really calm and easy to handle in here," Billy told Amy when she went up to him in the barn to say hi.

"Great!" said Amy.

"Rosie gave us Bonny's tack to try and she's happy with the fit, so we're ready to ride," Billy said. "She's going to be there to supervise, of course, but she's letting George take the lesson. Oh, here he is now."

"Hi, Amy. Where's Leah?" George asked, coming up to them. Amy was about to ask that question herself.

"She's tacking up Nutmeg," said Billy. He turned to Amy. "She's got Gracie in for you too, so we can all ride together."

"OK, I'll go and get her ready then," said Amy, her stomach flipping over with excitement.

"Billy and I will work with Spark on his own a bit first," George told them, "just to double-check he's OK for you to ride alongside. See you by the manège, yeah?"

About fifteen minutes later, Amy and Leah were standing by the manège gate, hats

118

on and ready to ride. Rosie stood in the
centre next to George, watching carefully as
Billy rode Spark around.

Spark had been a bit jumpy when Billy
first mounted up, but now they were
trotting happily, making turns and circles
and going from walk to trot and back again.
"He's definitely been ridden in the past,
before his back problem started," said Leah.

"Yeah," Amy agreed, "and he seems to
really enjoy it. He's bonding well with Billy
too."

After a few more minutes, George asked the girls to go in, so they collected Gracie and Nutmeg from the barn, and mounted up and all rode round together in walk. "Oh, this is weird!" Amy exclaimed, as she took Gracie on behind Spark. "I've never ridden in a group before."

"Just watch you don't get too close…" George warned. But it was too late – Amy had ridden Gracie too near to Spark's hindquarters, and he kicked out in protest then skittered across the manège.

"Don't panic, Billy, just bring him back to a nice walk," Rosie called.

Billy only just managed to keep his balance and not go tumbling off, but he soon regained control and got Spark back on to the track.

"Sorry!" Amy cried.

"Don't worry," George told her. "Lots of ponies get upset if people ride too close.

Hopefully he won't react as much when he gets used to having others around. But, Billy, maybe you should go at the back for now."

Rosie nodded. "I think that's a good idea," she said.

Billy led Spark to the back of the ride, leaving Amy at the front. But then she misheard an instruction to "trot" as a command to "stop" and Nutmeg went crashing into the back of Gracie, which sent Spark prancing across the manège again. After that she found herself getting nervous and constantly glancing round to check where Nutmeg was.

"Just worry about what *you're* doing," George told her. "Leah can handle Nutmeg."

"I'll try," said Amy, but she still had that nervous, panicky feeling for the rest of the practice. She couldn't even shake it off as they led their ponies back on to the yard, and Leah noticed that something was wrong.

"Don't worry about those little things," she told her, "you'll get used to riding in a group in time."

"But we don't *have* time," Amy told her. "And if I mess things up and spook Spark again in the demo on Saturday, your mum and dad might say no to him staying. Then Billy will never forgive me." She glanced at Leah, hoping she'd wave away her fears and say something positive. But Leah looked just as worried as she did.

The next day was Friday, and Amy finally got her chance to hack out on Gracie, but she didn't feel as excited about it any more, not since she'd had so much trouble riding with the other ponies in the manège. She'd told her mum all about the group lesson disaster the night before at teatime. Mum had just said she was sure everything would be fine and not to worry – but because she had no idea about ponies, it hadn't really helped.

Actually, though, it turned out she was right. Being out in the open was a whole different feeling from being confined in the manège. Rosie didn't have time to ride out in the end, so Dan took them. He rode behind Amy and kept a good distance, so she found that she didn't feel nervous about them crashing into each other.

George was in front on a grey mare called Ella and they didn't make any sudden stops, so Amy had a chance to practise keeping the right distance herself, too. Spark listened to Billy well, and hardly even reacted when two pheasants came stumbling out of a bush right in front of them. And when Leah opened a gate for them all and it clanged loudly as it shut, Spark didn't flinch any more than the other ponies either.

As they turned off the lane and up a farm

track, Amy was riding next to Leah, who was swinging her legs out of the stirrups and chatting. Everything was going so well they almost forgot that Spark was on trial, and that Dan would be reporting back to Rosie. That is, it was going well until a dog rushed out of a farm gate ahead of them, barking excitedly. They could all see it was friendly, but poor Spark kicked out and bolted off, and Billy only just managed to stay in the saddle. Dan didn't say anything about it, but he didn't look too happy.

"If Spark spooks like that during the demo, we'll have no chance," Billy said anxiously to the girls, as they made their way back to the yard. "Plenty of ponies would have spooked in that situation, but I know that Rosie won't be happy with it."

"Looks like it's just barking dogs that make Spark nervous now he's calmed down in general," said Leah. "Do you remember when we got him to the yard? He spooked when Rufus barked too. He was fine with those pheasants and the gate, though. We'll just have to get him used to the sound of barking – and quickly."

So as soon as they'd got back to the yard and untacked Nutmeg and Gracie, they got to work. Rosie and Jane headed out on a hack with a group of tourists but Dan didn't have any lessons to teach, so they asked him to supervise them.

Billy rode Spark round the track in the

manège, while Leah encouraged Rufus to run up and down by the fence, and fussed and tickled him to make him bark excitedly. Spark didn't like it, and he bolted off a couple of times, bucking across the manège. Dan didn't comment, but he kept a close eye on them. Despite their best efforts, Spark didn't seem to be getting any more used to Rufus. After a hot and dusty hour, they had to admit defeat – to do any more on the sunny afternoon wouldn't have been fair on Spark.

As Amy and Leah walked back to the farmhouse, Amy noticed her mum's car and realized with a start that it was already five o'clock. "Where on earth has the day gone?" she gasped. "Oh, I'm so worried about tomorrow, Leah. Spark's still nervous of dogs, even lovely Rufus. What if he bolts or rears up like that when your mum's watching? And your dad saw him do it this afternoon, anyway, so he's bound to tell her…"

Leah put her arm round her. "Don't worry! We've all done our best. We'll just have to make sure that noisy mutt of mine is kept in the house during the demo tomorrow."

Amy gave her an anxious look. "But what if I mess up the display and spook Spark? Maybe I should pretend to be ill or something… If I don't ride, I can't let Billy down."

Leah frowned. "Oh, please don't do that. Mum needs to see how Spark copes being in with a novice rider, or she won't be able to make a decision. And anyway, you were fine on that ride out – just tell yourself that being in the manège is no different."

"I'll try," said Amy, but she couldn't shake off her fear.

When they reached the farmhouse, Amy found her mum in the kitchen, chatting to Rosie. She grabbed her stuff, thanked Rosie

for having her and then gave Leah a big
goodbye hug.

"See you tomorrow," said Leah. "It'll be
OK, well, fingers crossed."

"See you," said Amy.

"How did it go with Spark today?" asked
Mum as they walked to the car.

Amy shrugged. "Fine, mostly. But I'm
really not sure which way it will go. He's
still got an issue with barking dogs and
Rosie will be tough to please."

"Quite right," said Mum. "She has to be
sure he's completely safe, darling. You can
understand that, can't you?"

"Yes," said Amy, getting into the car.

"I'm sure it will all be OK," said Mum.
"I'm coming to watch, too – I'm quite
looking forward to seeing you in action!"

Amy felt sick. That would be one more
person who'd see her mess the whole
thing up.

CHAPTER NINE

On Saturday morning, Amy and Leah were busy in the barn getting Gracie and Nutmeg ready for the demo, when Billy led Spark in, followed by his parents and Rosie.

"Look," said Billy, running a body brush over Spark's back, "not a problem."

Even Rosie was impressed by that and by how willingly Spark picked up his hooves to have them picked out.

"When you think how he wouldn't even let you near him before—" Leah began, but both Amy and Billy glared at her and she trailed off. They didn't want to advertise to Billy's parents exactly how bad Spark had been!

Soon, Billy's mum was stroking Spark's nose and his dad was feeding him a carrot. "He's a lovely pony," he said.

"You can see he's great to handle," said Amy.

"And he obviously likes you both too," Leah added. "He'd fit right into the family!"

"Hang on," said Rosie. "We—"

"...mustn't get ahead of ourselves," Leah, Amy and Billy chorused, and then burst into giggles.

Rosie couldn't help smiling. "Well, I'm happy that he's fine on the yard," she said. "Let's find out how he does with a rider, shall we? George is waiting for you all."

Amy, Leah and Billy looked at each other. Amy felt her stomach flipping over and over with a mix of nerves and excitement. This was it – the moment of truth. Time to see if all their hard work had paid off. And to find out whether Spark and Billy would be able to stay together. She felt a wave of panic rise up inside her. She really didn't want to ruin things for them.

They all filed into the manège, with Amy on Gracie at the back. She gave Mum a quick wave as she went by, and Mum waved back and then crossed her fingers. George got them to start walking round to warm up. Spark seemed a bit unsure about all the people standing by the manège fence when he had to walk past them, but luckily George's idea to put Leah and Nutmeg in front of him had worked. Spark seemed to take confidence from that and just followed on. That was a good start anyway! Billy glanced round, caught Amy's eye and grinned.

There was another unexpected test when Jane clattered by, pushing a wheelbarrow with two pitchforks balanced in it. Luckily, Spark only took a few steps away from it (as did Gracie) and let Billy guide him back on to the track with no problems.

As they trotted round, Amy concentrated hard on keeping Gracie back from Spark's hindquarters, while making sure she didn't lag behind either. She had one close call where she lost her stirrup, just when everyone was pulling their ponies up, and she could only stop Gracie inches from Spark. But luckily George saw what had happened and moved everyone back into trot quickly, so that Billy could ride Spark away before he got too upset.

Billy and Spark's showpiece, a nice controlled canter to the back of the ride, went so well that the crowd by the gate gave them a round of applause. Just before her go, Amy turned and grinned at him and he beamed back at her. Things had gone really well, and they were almost finished. But then, "Oh no!" Leah hissed, waving an arm towards the farmhouse. "Look! Who let *him* out?"

Amy turned to see Rufus bounding across the yard. He had clearly spotted Leah and was making for the manège. "Go away, boy!" Leah hissed. "You'll ruin everything!"

But instead of going away, Rufus had clearly decided that he must be needed again for pony-training duty and ran up and down beside the manège, barking with excitement. Spark began to get restless and skitter about.

"Oh, no, here we go!" said Billy, gritting his teeth.

"Keep him focused on Leah and Nutmeg and ride strongly forward," called George.

Billy looked determinedly ahead and rode on, but Amy could see that he'd tensed up completely.

"Sorry!" Rosie was saying to Amy's mum and Billy's parents. "Rufus has never done this before."

"I'll grab him," said Dan, frowning.

But Rufus thought that having Dan running about after him was a great game and gave him the slip every time, while still bouncing about by the fence, barking merrily. Spark gave a little buck and then a bigger one. Amy held her breath, waiting for him to go crazy across the manège and dump Billy on the ground.

Rosie would definitely say no to keeping him if she saw that.

But to Amy's amazement, that didn't happen. Instead, Billy spoke soothingly to Spark, and rode him confidently forward. After a while, the pony began to calm down. "Well done, that's brilliant, just keep going!" Amy called out.

"Thanks!" Billy called back.

Dan finally got hold of Rufus and stopped him barking.

"Now let your reins out so your ponies can have a good stretch," George called. "Well done, everyone."

The group by the fence gave them a big clap as they dismounted, and then came into the manège to join them.

"Well done, son, you rode really well, and this fella tried very hard," said Billy's dad, as he and his mum both made a big fuss of Spark.

"You were amazing, love!" Mum told Amy.

"Thanks," said Amy. She looked anxiously over at Dan and Rosie, who were talking together by the fence. "I just hope we've done enough to convince them."

"Me too," said Leah. "We weren't exactly perfect, and that thing with Rufus…" Just then, she spotted Adam slipping under the manège fence. "Oy! You let him out, didn't you?" she accused.

Adam grinned cheekily at her. "Didn't you want him out, then?" he asked.

"You know I didn't, you little toerag!" Leah cried. "If you've ruined this for Billy, I'll—"

"Ahem! I'm sure you'd like to know what Dan and I think," said Rosie, striding up to the group. "Well, look, it wasn't perfect... Much more work needs to be done with Spark..."

Billy and the girls shared a worried glance. What did that mean? Amy wondered. How much more work was too much? Was Rosie going to say no?

"But ponies are animals, not machines," Dan continued. "They all have some degree of unpredictability and perhaps Spark has a little more than most, but we feel that it's well within safe limits. And he'll be kept strictly for the advanced groups at first..." He broke off and looked at Rosie.

Amy stared at them, hardly daring to hope...

"Does that mean yes?" Leah asked.

Rosie smiled. "It means yes," she told them.

Amy wanted to go crazy then, hugging and jumping about, and she knew Leah did

too, but they didn't want to spook the
ponies, so they settled for a big clap and
cheer instead.

"Thank you," said Billy, beaming and
throwing his arms round Spark. Spark
whinnied right on cue, making them all
laugh, as if he was saying thank you too.

"Thank Adam," said Rosie with a grin. "Seeing how well Spark handled Rufus leaping about and barking like that really clinched it for me. Dan said he'd had real trouble coping with a barking dog on the ride out, and with Rufus being beside the manège yesterday, so this has really proved that he can learn and change his behaviour."

Leah smiled. So Adam hadn't wrecked things for them after all!

"We'd like to say a big well done to you, Leah and Amy, and to Billy and George," Rosie was saying. "You've worked really hard to help Spark. We're so proud of you."

"I second that," Billy's dad said.

Mum gave Amy a big hug.

"Right, well, I'll need you here at six on the dot tomorrow morning," Rosie told Billy.

"Six? But that's the middle of the night!" Billy gasped, making them all laugh.

"You'd better get used to early starts,"

said Rosie. "You'll have to work really hard to cover Spark's livery costs, and we'll need to get him his own tack, of course, which isn't cheap."

"I can always cover for you in an emergency," said Leah. "It would have to be a dire emergency mind, like your arm dropping off or something!"

"Thanks, Leah," said Billy, giving her a smile.

"Your arm *might* drop off," Dan told Billy, "with all the work Rosie's got planned for you!"

"I don't mind," Billy said. "So long as I've got Spark, and Spark's got me, that's all that matters. And me and Spark would like to thank you all for making it possible ... especially Amy and Leah ... and Rufus!"

Amy grinned at Leah as everyone clapped them. Then, as they all headed out of the manège, Rosie said, "Right, I'll go and call the rescue charity now, and Anna, of course, to tell her the good news."

As she strode off towards the office, Leah said to Amy, "Why is it that the one bit of training I didn't want Rufus to remember, running up and down barking his head off, is the one thing that stuck?"

Amy giggled. "Maybe you should try reverse training in future," she suggested. "You know, tell him what you *don't* want him to do."

"Good thinking," said Leah. "Rufus, *don't* sit!" she commanded. But he just looked at her, puzzled.

"Oh well!" said Amy. "It was worth a go!"

As they watched Billy lead Spark back out of the manège, Leah added, "Now Spark's got a new life in a new place with his perfect new owner. I'd call that another great result for Animal S.O.S.!"

"Me too," said Amy, with a grin. "And it's only the start of the summer. Who knows how many exciting animal adventures are in store for us!"

To find out more about Kelly McKain,
visit her website:

www.kellymckain.co.uk